# FAR EAST STORIES
## FOR PLEASURE READING

*By*

EDWARD W. DOLCH
MARGUERITE P. DOLCH
BEULAH F. JACKSON

*Illustrated by*

FRANCISCO MIDDLE SCHOOL
SIP
1990–1991

DLM
Teaching
Resources
One DLM Park • Allen, Texas 75002

# Foreword

Long ago, when the people of Europe began to hear of the countries to the east of them, they learned of some countries far away which they then called the Far East. That is why we now speak of China and Japan and other countries near them as being part of the Far East.

The Far East has always been the land of stories and of men who made their living by story telling. Each of the countries has a very great number of stories, some very old and some not so old. Some time you may read the many books of stories of these countries.

To give you a taste of the many interesting stories, we have selected a few from some of the countries of the Far East. The stories in this book are from China, Japan, Korea, Indonesia, Tibet, and India. These stories are told with all their old interest and charm, and will give you some idea of the tales from these Far Eastern countries.

E. W. DOLCH

Urbana, Illinois

# List of Pictures

# Contents

# The Blue Rose

Long, long ago, there lived in China an Emperor who was wise and good. He had one son and one daughter.

The son was a fine young man and he had a beautiful wife. They had a strong and beautiful baby boy. The old Emperor was very happy for he knew that there would be someone to take his place after he was dead.

But his daughter had not married.

The Emperor's daughter was the most beautiful girl in China. She had big brown eyes that would shine when she was happy like the water of the river when it runs over little stones. And when she laughed, it sounded like silver bells were ringing.

Many men had wanted to marry the Emperor's daughter. But she was as wise as she was beautiful. She had not found one man that she could love.

One day the Emperor called his daughter to him.

"My dear daughter," said the Emperor. "I am getting old. Before I die, I want to see you married."

"Yes, my Father, I want to marry some one as good and as wise as you are," said the Emperor's daughter.

Soon it became known that the Emperor was looking for someone to marry his daughter. One hundred young men came to his palace and asked for her hand.

The Emperor went to his daughter and said,

"My daughter, the finest young men in the country have come to ask for your hand. Now which one of them do you want to marry?"

The Emperor's daughter thought for

a long time and then she said to her father,

"I will marry the one who brings me a blue rose."

When the young men heard what the Emperor's daughter had said, they looked at one another and said,

"A blue rose? Who ever heard of a blue rose? There is no such thing as a blue rose." And all but three of the young men went home.

One of the three who stayed was a very rich young man. He went to a flower store in the city where you could buy many, many kinds of flowers. He went to the man who owned the store and said,

"I want to buy a blue rose, the largest one you have."

The man who owned the flower store bowed very low and said,

"I am very sorry but I have no blue

roses. I have red roses and yellow roses and white roses. But I have no blue roses."

"Find me a blue rose," said the rich young man. "And if you do not find me a blue rose, I will have your head cut off."

The man who owned the flower shop was very much afraid and he said, "Just give me three days and I will find a blue rose for you."

The rich young man went away. And the man who owned the flower shop ran home to his wife. He told her everything that had happened.

"Oh, what shall I do?" he cried. "There is no such thing as a blue rose, and in three days the rich young man will come back and cut off my head."

"We will make a blue rose," said his wife. "Go and bring me some strong blue color and a large white rose. I will make the white rose into a blue rose."

When the wife had made the white rose into a blue rose, the shop keeper took it to the rich young man. The rich young man was well pleased and he took the blue rose to the Emperor's palace.

When the Emperor saw that the rich young man had brought a blue rose, he called his daughter and said,

"This rich young man has brought you a blue rose. Is that what you wanted?"

The Emperor's daughter was very wise. She took the blue rose in her little hands.

"This is a white rose that has been colored blue," said the Emperor's daughter. "If a butterfly or a bird would light upon this rose, the blue color would kill it. I have no use for this kind of a rose."

The rich young man took his blue

rose and went away. He was very angry for he had wanted to marry the Emperor's daughter.

One of the three young men who wanted to marry the Emperor's daughter was a soldier. He called out one thousand of his best soldiers. They got on their horses and rode to the country of the King of the Five Rivers. This king was the richest king in all the world. Everyone knew that he had the finest things that could be found anywhere.

The soldiers rode up to the palace of the King of the Five Rivers. The King heard them coming and sent his servants to ask what they wanted.

The soldier said to the King's servants, "Go and tell the King that we have come for the blue rose. If he does not give it to me, my men will take it."

The servants went back and told the

King what the soldier wanted. And the King said to his servants,

"Go and get the blue rose and give it to the soldier. Tell the soldier to take his men away. We want no fighting and killing here."

The servants went away and brought back a beautiful blue rose that had been cut out of a blue stone. It was on a white silk pillow. The soldier thought that it was the most beautiful thing that he had ever seen.

The soldier rode off to the Emperor's palace. When the Emperor saw that the soldier had brought a blue rose, he called his daughter and said,

"This soldier has brought you a blue rose. Is this what you wanted?"

The Emperor's daughter was very wise. She took the blue rose in her little hands and she looked at it very closely.

"This is not a rose," said the Emperor's daughter. "This is a beautiful blue stone cut to look like a rose. I have many beautiful stones. I will give this one back to you for you think that it is the most beautiful thing in the world."

The soldier got on his horse and rode away. He was very angry for he had wanted to marry the Emperor's daughter.

The third young man was a very wise man. He sent for a painter, the very best painter in the whole country.

"Make me a cup," said the wise young man. "Make me the most beautiful cup in the world. And paint a blue rose upon the cup."

The painter worked for three months. When he had finished the cup, he brought it to the wise young man.

The cup was white and on it was painted a blue rose, so beautiful that it looked like a real rose. The wise young man was very happy and he paid the painter well. Then he hurried to the Emperor's palace.

When the Emperor saw that the wise young man had brought a blue rose, he called his daughter and said,

"This young man has brought you a beautiful blue rose. Is this what you wanted?"

"You are wise and you are kind," said the Emperor's daughter. "You have brought me the most beautiful cup that I have ever seen. I would like to keep it. When someone brings me a blue rose, I shall put it in this beautiful cup."

The wise young man went away and he was very sad. The Emperor's daughter was very beautiful and he loved her very much. But the Emperor's daughter did not love him.

# The Blue Rose Is Found

The Emperor's daughter has said she would marry the man who brought her a blue rose. Three young men had tried to find the blue rose for her, but what they brought only looked like blue roses. She had turned them away.

Not long after that, just as the sun was going down, a young man walked by the Emperor's garden. This young man was a singer of songs. He sang of the beautiful colors in the sky. He sang of the soft night coming on. He sang of the sound of the river as it ran over the stones. He sang of the goodness of the Emperor and how beautiful was the Emperor's daughter.

As the young man stood there singing the songs that were in his heart, the garden gate opened.

A beautiful girl asked him to come into the garden.

The young man and the beautiful girl walked in the garden and they talked of many things. They talked of the beautiful sky. They talked of the soft night. They talked of the sound of the river. And they talked of each other. And the girl knew that she would love this young man for ever and ever.

"If you would marry the Emperor's daughter," said the girl, "you must find a blue rose."

"But I do not want to marry the Emperor's daughter," said the young man, "I want to marry you."

"Ah, me. I am the Emperor's daughter," said the beautiful girl. "And I said that I would marry only the man who brought me a blue rose."

"I will go and find one," said the

young man. "And I will bring it to you in the morning."

When the sun was coming up, the singer of songs went out into the country. He sang of the sun coming up over the mountains. He sang of the birds in the trees. And he sang of his love for the beautiful daughter of the Emperor. As he walked along, he saw a beautiful white rose beside the road. The lovely rose made him think of the princess. This rose must be for her. So he picked the big white rose that grew by the road. And then he went back to the Emperor's palace.

"Wise and good Emperor," said the young man. "I am a singer of songs that will never die. I have come to marry your daughter, for I love her very much. I bring her this beautiful blue rose."

The Emperor called his daughter and said,

"This singer of songs says that he has brought you a blue rose. Is this what you wanted?"

The Emperor's daughter took the beautiful white rose in her little hands. She looked at the rose and she looked at the young man.

"Yes," she said. "This is what I wanted. I can see that the singer of songs has brought me the blue rose."

Then all the people in the palace came to look at the rose.

"This is not a blue rose," they said. "This is only a white rose that grows in the country by the side of the road."

The Emperor thought of the rich young man who had brought a rose with blue color on it. He thought of the soldier who had brought a beautiful blue stone cut like a rose. He thought of the wise young man who had the painter make a beautiful cup and paint upon it a blue rose that would last forever.

Then the Emperor looked at his daughter. He knew that she was as wise as she was beautiful. The singer of songs was the man his daughter loved.

The Emperor held up his hand and said,

"If the Emperor's daughter says that the rose is blue, it must be a blue rose."

So the Emperor's daughter and the singer of songs that would never die were married. They lived happily ever after in a beautiful house set in a garden of white roses.

# The Magic Pillow

One day, an old Chinese priest stopped at an Inn beside the road and sat down under a tree to rest. He put his bag down beside him on the grass and lay back against the tree. Through the open door, he could see the Innkeeper cooking in the kitchen. The priest thought he would rest under the tree until the dinner was ready.

He had not been there long before a young farmer came by. He saw the priest sitting with his back against the tree and so the young farmer came and sat down in the grass beside him. Soon they were talking and having a fine visit.

The young man had just come from working in the fields. By and by, he looked down at the dirty clothes he was wearing.

"I am surely a sorry-looking fellow," he said.

"You look all right to me," said the priest. "You look as though you had enough to eat, and enough to wear, and enough work to do. You look as if you should be happy. What more could you wish for?"

"Why, I'm not a bit happy!" cried the young man. "I get up early and I work all day. I get dirty and hot and tired. I would like to be a great soldier and lead my men to war. Or I would like to be a rich man and have nice clothes to wear and fine food to eat. Or I would like to be so very wise that I could help our Emperor rule the country. That is the kind of a life that I would like."

"You look to me as well off as any-one I have seen in the whole country," said the priest.

"But don't you see that I am just a poor farmer," said the young man. "I am dressed in dirty clothes. I wonder what makes you think that I am happy."

The priest did not answer. He looked in at the kitchen door and saw that the Innkeeper did not have dinner ready.

Then the priest reached into his bag and took out a piece of wood such as the people of China used as a pillow when they went to sleep. He gave the pillow to the young farmer.

"Young man, take a nap on my magic pillow. While you sleep, all your dreams will come true," said the priest.

Now the pillow was round and it just fit the young man's neck and shoulders. He was hot and tired and so he lay down in the grass and put his head upon the pillow. He went right to sleep.

He dreamed that he was in his own house and that he was married to a beautiful girl. Then they went away to live in the city. He lived in a big house. He wore nice clothes and he had fine food to eat.

Then the young man saw himself as a soldier. He was sitting on a great horse and leading his men into the fight. But the next thing, his men were carrying him into his own house. His wife was crying. He knew that he was badly hurt and for many months he lay in bed.

While the young man lay sick in his bed, he read many, many big books. And at the end of a year he was so wise that the Emperor asked him to be his chief helper. And the young man and his beautiful wife were very happy.

Then something went wrong. He and his wife were in a great hall before many people. The Emperor was very, very angry. He said that the young man and his wife must be killed. The man who kills people came with a long, sharp knife. The knife was coming down on his neck. The young man was so afraid that he let out a great cry and opened his eyes.

There he was in the grass beside the Inn. There sat the old priest against the tree. Inside the door, the Innkeeper was still cooking, and the dinner was not quite ready.

The young man got up and bowed low before the old priest.

"Thank you, kind Sir, for letting me use your magic pillow," he said. "I have learned many things in my short nap. I know what it would be like to be a great man. And I know that I would rather be a happy farmer."

With that, he said goodbye to the priest and went back to his work in the field.

# The Pear Tree

Now it is said that there is magic in China, and a very great magic it is. This is a story of magic.

One day a farmer from the country was selling pears at the market. He had a cart full of pears. He was selling them for much money, for the pears were big, and the pears were sweet.

By and by, a priest came along. He was dressed in rags, and he looked like a poor old man. He stopped by the farmer's cart and asked him for one of the pears.

"My good man," said the priest. "I have walked a long way today and I am very tired. I would like one of your pears to eat."

But when the farmer saw that the priest had no money to pay for a pear, he told the old priest to go away.

The priest did not go away. He just stood there waiting for the farmer to give him a pear.

The farmer became very angry. He picked up a stick and tried to drive the priest away.

"I will not give you one of my pears. Go away" he said. "Go away."

"Why do you get so angry?" said the priest. "You have two hundred pears in your cart. I want only one pear. You have so many pears. You would not miss the one you gave to me."

"Be off with you," cried the farmer. "I will not give you one of my pears."

It was then that the people in the market place came to see what was the matter. They felt sorry for the poor priest.

"Give the priest a pear," said one man. "Don't give him the best pear that you have. Give him a small pear and then he will go away."

But the farmer was angry and he would not give the priest even a small pear.

Pretty soon all the people were talking at once. Some of the people thought that the farmer ought to give the priest a pear. Some of the people thought that the priest ought to go away. Some of the people began to fight about it. Then a man took some money out of his own pocket and gave it to the farmer for one of his pears. This pear he gave to the priest.

The priest bowed very low and thanked the man. Then, turning to the crowd of people, he said,

"We priests travel around doing good to others. We cannot understand people who act as this farmer does. I, myself, have many fine pears. And I will give them all to you."

Then one man in the crowd called out,

"If you have many pears, why did you not eat them instead of asking the farmer for one of his pears?"

"Because," answered the priest, "I wanted the seeds from one of the farmer's pears to grow some pears for you."

The people watched the priest eat the pear. When he had finished eating the pear, he made a hole in the ground. Then he took the seeds from the pear and put them into the hole in the ground. And the people watched.

"Now," said the priest to one of the men who was watching him, "Please bring me some warm water. I want to water my pear tree."

The man went and got some very hot

water from a woman who lived near by. The man thought that the very hot water would kill the pear seeds that the priest had put into the hole in the ground.

The priest took the hot water and put it on the ground where he had planted the pear seeds.

The people watched. They thought they saw a little green leaf come through the ground. The green leaf grew and grew. More leaves came. And soon a small tree stood there. It grew and grew. Soon it was covered with flowers. The flowers dropped off. Then the tree was covered with little green pears. The little green pears grew and grew. They turned to big yellow pears.

The people thought they saw the priest walk up to the tree and pick the big yellow pears. The priest put the big sweet pears into their hands and they all began to eat. And as the people were eating the pears, they thought they saw the priest pull up the pear tree. He put it upon his shoulder. Then the priest walked off down the road.

Now the farmer had been in the crowd of people around the priest all of this time. He forgot all about his cart and his pears. He even ate one of the pears the priest handed him and he thought it tasted a lot like one of his own pears.

After the priest had gone down the road, the farmer looked around for his cart. He saw his cart but there were no pears in it . All the pears were gone and his cart was empty.

Then the farmer knew that the old priest had used his magic on them. He had made them think that a pear tree was growing in the market place. He had made them see big yellow pears growing on the pear tree. But the pears the old priest had given the people were the pears out of the farmer's cart.

The farmer was very angry. He ran down the road after the priest. But he never found him.

And the crowd of people in the market place ate their pears and laughed and laughed at the farmer.

This is a story about the magic of China. And a very great magic it is.

# The Boy Who Painted Cats

A long, long time ago in a little town in Japan there lived a poor farmer and his wife. They had to work hard for a living. They had many children. And as soon as the children were big enough, they, too, had to work on the farm. Everyone in the family worked on the farm except the youngest son.

The youngest son could learn things very quickly. But he did not grow as his brothers and sisters did. He was very small. And his father and his mother knew that he could never work on the farm as the others did.

One night after all the children were in bed, the father and the mother talked about their youngest son.

"I do not think that our youngest son will ever be a farmer," said the father.

"No," said the mother. "He will always be small. He is not strong enough to be a farmer. But he can learn quickly and he likes to paint pictures. Do you suppose the old priest would take him for a helper? Then our youngest son could learn to be a priest."

"Tomorrow we will take him to the temple," said the father. "We will ask the old priest if he will take our youngest son for a helper."

The next day the farmer and his wife took their little boy to the temple. They asked the old priest if he would take the boy for a helper and teach him to be a priest.

"Let me talk to the boy a little while," said the old priest.

The old priest asked the little boy many questions. And the boy could think so fast that he answered every one. The priest was well pleased and told the father and the mother that he would keep the little boy and teach him to be a priest.

The father and the mother went back to their farm. They were very happy that their youngest son was going to become a priest.

The little boy was very happy in the temple. He learned his lessons very easily and he did his work very quickly. But he was always doing one thing that he was not supposed to do. He liked to paint pictures of cats.

He painted cats on the walls of the temple. He painted cats on the doors and the windows. He painted cats on the floors. He painted cats on the tables and the chairs. He painted cats on his books and on the old priest's books.

The old priest was very kind to the little boy.

"Be a good little boy," said the old

priest. "It is wrong to paint cats on everything. Do not paint any more cats."

But the little boy could not stop painting cats.

One day the old priest got a new screen for his house. The screen was covered with white silk. That day the little boy got through his lessons very quickly. And when he saw the new screen, he went and got his brush and his ink. Then he painted cats all over the screen.

He painted little cats and big cats. He painted laughing cats and sad cats. He painted running cats and fighting cats. He painted cats in houses and cats up in trees. And then the kind old priest came in.

"My boy," said the old priest, "I am afraid that I will have to send you home. You spend all of your time painting pictures of cats. Some day you may be a great painter but you will never be a priest. Get your things now and go home to your father and mother."

The little boy was very sad. He knew that he had been a bad boy to paint cats on the priest's new screen. He put his clothes in a bag and got ready to go home. Just before he left, the old priest spoke to him again.

"Let me tell you one more thing," said the old man. "Never sleep in large places. Always sleep in small places and you will be safe. And now Goodbye."

The little boy said goodbye and walked away. He did not want to go home. He knew that his father and his mother would be very sorry that he was not going to be a priest.

Then he remembered that he had heard that there was another temple in the next town. Perhaps the priests there would need a helper. The little boy put his bag on his back and walked to the next town.

It was dark when he got to the town, and all the people were asleep. But the little boy found the temple. It was a very large temple. He could see a light in the temple and so he walked up to the door and knocked.

No one came to the door.

The little boy knocked again.

This time the door of the temple opened but the little boy could see no one. He could see a light burning on a table. The little boy went into the temple and sat down by the table. He thought that the priest would soon come.

The little boy did not know that there were no priests in the temple. He did not know that a Goblin that looked like a rat but that was as big as a horse had come to live in the temple. The Goblin put a light in the temple each night. He wanted some one to come to the temple so that he could eat him.

Many soldiers had come to drive the Goblin out of the temple so that the priests could come back. The soldiers marched into the temple. And no one ever saw one of them again. And now no one in the town ever came to the temple.

The little boy did not know all of these things. He just sat and waited and waited. But no one came. He looked around him and he saw that everything was covered with dust.

"These priests need a boy to work for them," said the little boy to himself. "Perhaps they will let me stay."

Then the little boy saw a very large screen. It was the largest screen that he had ever seen. And it was covered with white silk.

"What a wonderful place to paint

cats," thought the little boy. Then he saw that there was a brush and some ink on the table. Without stopping to think, he began to paint cats on the large screen.

Now since the little boy was afraid in the big dusty room, he did not paint any little happy cats. He painted big, strong, fighting cats with long teeth. He painted and he painted and he painted. He must have painted a hundred big, strong cats before he got so sleepy that he could not keep his eyes open any longer.

Just as he was going to lie down beside the screen and go to sleep, he remembered what the old priest had said, "Never sleep in large places. Always sleep in small places and you will be safe."

The little boy looked all around. He opened door after door and he saw rooms that were bigger than the one he was in. At last he opened a little door and found a small cupboard. There was just enough room for him to lie down. He lay down in the cupboard and pulled the door shut. Soon he was fast asleep.

Very late in the night, the little boy heard a loud noise. It sounded like a hundred cats fighting. He was so afraid that he could not move. He just shut his eyes and made himself very small.

The noise got louder and louder. The whole temple seemed to be shaking. The little boy was so afraid that he did not know what to do. He just lay in the cupboard as still as a mouse.

By and by the noise died down. Pretty soon, it was quiet again. But still the little boy was afraid to move. He lay there in the cupboard for a long, long time. He began to get very hungry. And he wanted a drink of water.

At last he opened his eyes. He opened the door just a little way. All was quiet. He opened the door of the cupboard and looked out.

There on the floor of the temple lay a great rat as big as a horse. He was as dead as he could be.

But who had killed the Goblin Rat? There was no one in the temple.

Then the little boy looked at the big fighting cats that he had painted on the screen. He had painted them all with black ink. But now their mouths and their long teeth were red.

Then he knew that the hundred fighting cats that he had painted on the screen had killed the Goblin Rat.

And oh, how glad he was that he had remembered the words of the old priest, "Never sleep in large places. Always sleep in small places and you will be safe." For if he had gone to sleep beside the screen, the Goblin Rat would have killed him.

When the priests heard that the Goblin Rat had been killed, they came back to the temple at once. The little boy stayed with them. The priests were so thankful that they did not have the little boy work at all. He just painted cats.

Everyone in Japan knows about the boy who painted nothing but cats. Some of his pictures can be seen there to this day.

# The Story of Kogi, the Priest

Once upon a time, more than a thousand years ago, there lived in Japan a priest named Kogi. He painted beautiful pictures of animals and birds and trees and flowers. But he liked best to paint pictures of fish.

Kogi was getting very old, and one day he became sick. The doctor was called, but Kogi did not get better. In a short time, he could not talk or eat or move at all.

Then one morning when the other priests came to his room, they thought Kogi was dead. They were very sad because such a wonderful painter was dead. They carried him to the temple and lighted a lamp above his head.

The young priests sat beside the body

of Kogi. And one of the priests thought he saw the body of Kogi move.

"Perhaps Kogi is not dead," he said. "Perhaps we should watch over him a little while." And so the young priests put the body of Kogi on a bed in the temple. They watched beside the bed for three days.

Near evening of the third day, Kogi opened his eyes and looked around. He could see that he was in the temple. "How long have I been here?" he asked a young priest who sat beside the bed.

"Three days," said the young priest. "We were not sure that you were dead. We thought that we had better watch beside you for a while. Now we are very glad that we did."

"I, too, am glad," said Kogi. And he sat up in the bed. "Go to the house of the young men Suki and Juro. Their cook has cooked a large fish for them.

They are having a big dinner. Tell them to come to the temple at once for I have a story to tell them."

The young priest ran to the house of Suki and Juro. He told them that Kogi was alive and wished to see them. The young men left their dinner and went to the temple.

Kogi smiled at them and said, "My friends, please answer some questions that I am going to ask you. First of all, did you buy a fish today from a fisherman named Bunshi?"

"Why, yes," said Suki. "But how did you know?"

"That fisherman, Bunshi, came to your door today with a fish three feet long in his basket," said Kogi. "It was in the afternoon and you two brothers were playing a game. Your servant, Komori, was watching you and eating some fruit. Is that true?"

"Yes, that is true," said Juro, very much surprised.

The old priest went on.

"Komori came to the door to talk to the fisherman. When he saw the big fish, he wanted to buy it. But the fish cost more money than he had. He talked to Bunshi and at last Bunshi sold him the fish for what money he had and a plate of fruit. Is that true?"

"Yes, Yes," said Suki and Juro together.

"After you all had looked at the beautiful fish," said Kogi, "you called the cook. You told the cook to cut up the fish and cook it for your dinner. And you were eating the fish when I sent the young priest to tell you to come to the temple."

"It happened just as you have said," said Suki.

"You have been in the temple for

three days as quiet as though you were dead," said Juro. "How could you know these things?"

"I will tell you my story," said the old priest. "Three days ago, I was awakened early in the morning. I felt very warm. I wanted to get some fresh air and so I got out of bed, or so it seemed to me, and walked down to the sea.

"This may have been a dream, but I became very light. I could move easily as a bird flies or as a fish swims. It was very warm and I wanted to go in swimming. You all know that I am not a very good swimmer. But when I jumped into the water, I could swim like a fish.

"I saw many beautiful fish around me and under me. I said to myself that I wish that I could swim like a fish to the bottom of the sea. And at that very minute a big golden fish said to me, 'I will make your wish come true.'

"I was turned into a big golden fish. And I went with many other fish to the bottom of the sea. And there I saw the King of the Sea.

" 'Kogi,' said the King of the Sea. 'You have always been kind to the fish. You have never killed a fish and you have never eaten a fish. And now I have turned you into a golden fish so that you can swim to the bottom of the sea. Remember that you must not eat any food made of fish no matter how good it may smell. And do not let the fisherman catch you.'

"Oh, what a wonderful time I had. At the bottom of the sea there are beautiful colored sea flowers and beautiful colored fish. Sometimes I would come up to the top of the water and watch the sunlight dance over the blue waves. Then I would swim down to the cool dark green at the bottom of the sea. Sometimes at night I would come to the top of the water. The moon was shining. I would swim down the silver path that the moon made on the sea.

"After three days of swimming in the sea, I became very hungry. I came to the top of the water just as fisherman Bunshi put down his fish line with fish food on it. And without thinking, I ate the fish food.

"Just as I did so, Bunshi pulled on his line. Up I came out of the water and into his boat.

" 'Stop,' I cried as loud as I could, 'Stop, you are hurting me.' But Bunshi did not seem to hear me. He put me in his basket and carried me to the house of the two brothers, Suki and Juro.

"When he took the top off of the

basket, I saw Suki and Juro playing a game. I saw the servant Komori eating fruit. I listened while Komori talked to Bunshi about how much he should pay for me.

"All the while I was saying as loud as I could, 'I am not a fish. I am Kogi. I am Kogi, the priest. Please take me back to the temple.'

"But you did not listen to me. Instead you seemed very happy to get such a large fish.

"The cook came and took me to the kitchen. He put me down hard on the table. I saw in his hand a long knife. Then Oh how loudly I cried,

'Do not kill me. Do not kill me. I am Kogi. I am Kogi, the priest. Help! Help! Help!'

"Down came the knife. I closed my eyes. Oh, I have never felt such pain. Then I opened my eyes and I was in this temple."

When the priest came to the end of his story, the brothers Suki and Juro were so surprised that they could hardly talk.

At last Suki said, "I remember seeing the mouth of the big fish moving all the time we were looking at it. But I did not hear anything."

"I can never eat fish out of the sea again," said Juro.

Kogi soon got well and painted many more pictures of the fish that he had seen in his dream. They were more beautiful than any he had painted before.

And some people say that once one of Kogi's pictures of fish fell into the sea. A big golden fish came and played with the fish in the picture. The fish in the picture were so real that they went swimming right off of the picture and down to the bottom.

# The Story of Hoichi

At Donnoura in Japan, there is a temple that looks out to the sea. And there is a burying ground beside the temple where there are great stones with names on them. But no one is buried there. And in the temple there once lived an old priest, and a boy who was blind.

The boy's name was Hoichi. And no one in all Japan could play on the biwa and sing the songs that tell of the great fight of Donnoura like the blind Hoichi.

In the evening, the priest could tell Hoichi again and again of the great fight of Donnoura. It was more than seven hundred years ago that the soldiers of Heike and the soldiers of Genji fought for days and days. At last the soldiers of Genji drove the soldiers of Heike into the sea.

The soldiers of Genji drove all the women and children into the sea too. And there was no one left of the family of Heike. The saddest part of the story was where the beautiful Empress took her little boy in her arms, — he was the boy Emperor — and jumped into the sea.

For hundreds and hundreds of years the spirits of those who had died in the sea had had no place to rest. Then the priests of Donnoura built the temple looking out to the sea. And in the burying ground beside the temple a stone was placed for each man and woman and child that had died in the great fight. And that is how the spirits of the family of Heike found a resting place.

As the old priest told the stories, Hoichi played on his biwa. You could hear the soldiers fighting. You could hear the cries of the people thrown into the sea. You could hear the spirits of the dead crying there was no place where they could rest. And when Hoichi played the story of the beautiful Empress with the boy Emperor in her arms who jumped into the sea, there were tears in the eyes of the old priest.

One night, the priest was called away to the house of a sick man. It was a very dark night. The servant went along with him carrying a light to show him the way. That left Hoichi all alone in the temple.

It was a very warm night. So Hoichi went out on a little porch which was outside his bedroom. It was nice and cool there. Hoichi sat there and played on the biwa and waited for the priest to come back.

Hoichi played a long, long time. And

still the priest did not come back. Hoichi got tired of playing. It was still very warm in his room. And so he sat outside quietly in the darkness.

Then Hoichi heard the sound of some steps coming toward him. Hoichi's ears had to tell him many things because his eyes could not. And he knew that these steps coming toward him were not the steps of the old priest.

"Hoichi," a loud voice called.

Hoichi was so surprised that he could not speak. Then the voice called again even more loudly,

"Hoichi."

"Yes," said Hoichi. "I am here. Who are you? I am blind, you know, so I cannot see you."

"Do not be afraid," said a man's voice. "I have been sent to ask you to do something. My Master has many guests with him tonight. They have heard that you sing of the great fight of Donnoura. They wish you to come and sing for them."

Now in those days, the wishes of a great man were not put aside by a poor boy like Hoichi. He put on his shoes, took up his biwa, and went with the man.

As soon as they were in the street, the man took the blind boy's hand and they walked very fast. Hoichi knew from the sounds that the man made when he walked, that he must be a soldier.

At last they stopped and the soldier cried, "Open the gate."

Hoichi heard the sounds of a big gate opening. They walked across some grass and stopped again.

The soldier cried, "You who are within. I have come back with Hoichi!"

A door opened and Hoichi heard the

voices of women talking together. From what they said, Hoichi guessed they were servants in some great house.

Hoichi did not know of any such great house near the temple. But he did not have time to wonder about it, for the servants took him into a big room and he heard the voices of many people.

Then Hoichi heard a woman's voice say, "My son wishes to hear you sing about the great fight of Donnoura."

Hoichi began to play his biwa and sing. He sang about the great fight beside the sea. You could hear the soldiers fighting. You could hear the cries of the people thrown into the sea.

All around him, Hoichi could hear the people talking. One said, "I have never heard such music." Another said, "There is not another boy in Japan that can play and sing like this."

This pleased Hoichi so much that he

played the best he had ever played in his life. After the song of the great fight, he sang about the death of the beautiful young women and the children. He sang about the mother of the Emperor who took the boy Emperor in her arms and jumped into the sea.

Then all the people cried. Louder and louder they cried until Hoichi had to stop playing.

When all was quiet, Hoichi heard the woman's voice saying,

"We did not know that anyone could sing and play as you do. Our Master is well pleased. He wishes you to come and sing for him every night for six nights. Then he must leave. But he will pay you well before he leaves. However, he does not want anyone to know about his visit. Tell no one what you have done tonight."

Hoichi bowed low and thanked her, for she had the voice of a great lady.

"You may go back to your temple now," said the great lady. "Tomorrow night someone will come for you again."

Then the soldier who had brought Hoichi, took him by the hand and led him back to the temple. He left him on the little porch outside his bedroom. Hoichi was very tired. He went into his room and went right to sleep.

No one knew that Hoichi had been gone from the temple. The priest and his servant had come back very late and thought that he was in bed asleep.

The next night the soldier came for Hoichi. And Hoichi went with him. He sang for the people again.

But in the night a storm came up. The old priest went to Hoichi's bedroom to close the windows. Hoichi was not in his bed. The priest waited and waited for Hoichi and when at last Hoichi came, the old priest said,

"My little friend, I have been afraid something had happened to you. It is not safe for a blind boy to be out on the streets this late at night. Tell me where have you been?"

Hoichi felt sorry that he could not tell the priest where he had been, so he said,

"Do not be angry with me, kind friend. I had something to do that I could not do at any other time. And I cannot tell you about it."

The old priest was very much surprised. It was not a bit like Hoichi to keep anything from him. He began to be afraid that the spirits of the dead, who often came to Donnoura, had something to do with Hoichi's staying out at night.

# Hoichi Is Saved from the Spirits

Hoichi, the blind boy who lived in the temple, has been going at night to sing for the spirits of those who had died in the great battle of Donnoura. The priest had found out that Hoichi went from the temple at night, but he did not know where Hoichi went.

The old priest said to his servant, "Watch over Hoichi. Find out where he goes and do not let him get hurt."

So that night, the servant watched and saw Hoichi leave his bedroom. The servant took a light and followed him. But Hoichi went so fast that the servant could not keep up with him. Hoichi was soon lost in the night.

The servant went to the homes of all of Hoichi's friends. But he was not there. No one had seen him. It began to rain very hard. And so at last, the servant started back to the temple.

As the servant came near the burying ground he heard someone playing a biwa and singing loudly. He had heard that song before. He followed the sound, knowing that it would lead him to Hoichi.

The servant came to the big gate of the burying ground. He could see the spirit fires dancing around. And there was Hoichi, sitting on a stone, playing the biwa and singing of the great fight of Donnoura. And the rain was coming down all around.

"Hoichi," called the servant. But Hoichi did not seem to hear. He went right on playing and singing.

Then the servant ran to Hoichi and picked him up in his arms. The servant ran with him to the temple. He put Hoichi down before the old priest.

"Take off his wet clothes," said the priest. "Put him to bed, for the boy is very tired."

In the morning, Hoichi told the old priest what had happened.

"Hoichi, my poor boy," said the old priest. "You are in great danger. You have fallen into the hands of the spirits of Donnoura. You were not going to a great house to play before many people. My servant found you in the burying ground sitting on the stone of the boy Emperor, playing your biwa and singing in the rain. The spirits of the dead will surely kill you. I must think of some way to save you."

The old priest went into the temple and stayed a long time. When he came out he said to Hoichi,

"Now I know what must be done to

save you from the spirits of the dead."

The priest and his servant worked all day to get Hoichi ready for the night. They took their brushes and painted on Hoichi's skin words from the book of their gods.

When night came, they thought that they had every bit of Hoichi's skin covered with words. There were words on his hands and his face. There were words on his arms and his legs. Even the bottoms of his feet were covered with words.

Then the old priest said, "Hoichi, tonight I want you to sit on your porch as before. But do not say a word and do not move. The man will come as before and call your name. He will try and get you to go with him. If you go, the spirits of the dead will kill you. Do not call for help because no one can help you. Do not be afraid, for if you do not move or cry out, the spirits of the dead cannot hurt you."

When it was dark, Hoichi went out on his porch. He put his biwa beside him and he sat very still. Soon he heard the sound of foot-steps.

"Hoichi," a loud voice called. But Hoichi did not move.

"Hoichi," cried the loud voice a second time. But Hoichi did not answer.

"Hoichi, where are you," cried the voice a third time. Hoichi sat still as a stone.

Hoichi heard the sound of great feet coming closer to him. Hoichi was afraid but he did not move a finger.

Then Hoichi heard the voice saying, "Here is the biwa on the porch. But all I can see of the biwa player are two ears in the darkness. So that is why he did not answer. He had no mouth with which to answer. Well, if all I can see are two ears, then that is all that I can take to my master."

At that minute, Hoichi felt a great pain in his ears. It hurt him very badly, but he did not cry out or move. Then he heard the footsteps go away from the porch. At last he could hear them no more. But still Hoichi was afraid to move.

Soon the priest came with a light. There sat Hoichi just as he had left him, except that his ears were gone.

"Oh, my poor Hoichi! What is this?" cried the priest.

Hoichi began to cry. And then he told the old priest what had happened.

"I am so sorry," said the priest. "I should have been more careful. I let the servant paint the words on your head. I suppose he forgot to paint the words from the prayers on the back of your ears."

The old priest took care of Hoichi,
and he was soon well. The story of
what had happened to him went far and
wide. Many people came to hear him
play and sing. They left him money,
and Hoichi soon had a fine house and
good clothes.

But from that time on, he was called
Mimi-nashi-Hoichi, which means Hoichi-
without-Ears.

# The Mirror That Made Trouble

In a town in the north of Korea, lived Mr. Kim and his wife Cho. Mr. Kim had always wanted to go to the great city of Seoul. And one day he said to his wife,

"I have worked hard and saved my money and now I think that I will go and see the great city of Seoul."

His wife Cho and the three daughters bowed low before him and wished him a nice trip. And each asked that he bring her a present from the city of Seoul. The old Grandmother told him to be careful of his money, and the old Grandfather said, "Do not eat too much of the rich food or you will get sick."

"Keep the fire from going out," said Mr. Kim to his wife. "And at night be sure that the door is locked. If you hear a tiger on the roof, ring the big bell and the neighbors will come and drive it away. And if you hear the pigs crying in the night, be sure to call the neighbors. For a tiger likes to eat Korean pigs even better than he likes to eat Korean people."

When Mr. Kim got to the city of Seoul, he looked all around him. He had never seen so many people in all of his life. And he had never seen so many buildings. And when he went into the shops and found how much things cost, he was afraid that he would not have money enough to buy all the presents that his wife and daughters wanted.

At last he bought some red shoes like the girls wore in the city. Then he bought some silver rings and some ribbons to wear in the hair.

Then Mr. Kim bought a roll of beautiful silk for his wife. The man at the silk shop thought that he would have some fun with Mr. Kim who had come from the little town in the country.

"Do you see that shop across the way?" said the man in the silk shop. "Go in there and ask to see the 'round magic.' "

At once Mr. Kim went across the street and into the shop. He stood in front of a round thing like a moon. In it was a man's face. The face looked like one of Mr. Kim's neighbors. When he turned around hoping to see his neighbor, there was no one there. He looked into the "round magic" again and there was the face of his friend.

When Mr. Kim laughed, the other fellow laughed. When Mr. Kim made a face, the other fellow made a face. No matter how quickly Mr. Kim turned around, the other fellow was always gone.

Now Mr. Kim had never seen a mirror. He thought that the round thing that he looked into was "round magic." He bought the mirror with all the money that he had left.

When Mr. Kim got back to his home, he gave his wife and daughters the presents that he had bought for them in the great city of Seoul. And then he went out to see how his pigs and his cows were getting along.

After the girls had looked at their pretty presents, they saw a box that their father had left on the table. They opened it and took out the mirror.

"Mother, Mother," called one of the daughters, "Come here and see the young girl that father brought home from Seoul."

Cho came running and looked into the mirror.

"It is another woman," she cried.

"To think that your father would bring another woman into my house."

And Cho began to cry. She cried so loudly that the Grandmother came running to see what was the matter.

The Grandmother looked into the mirror.

"Go away, old woman," she cried, "My son has enough people to look after without you coming to live with us."

Then the Grandmother began to cry. And she cried so loudly that the Grandfather came running to see what was the matter.

"What is all of that noise about?" asked the Grandfather.

The daughters tried to tell him. Cho, the wife, tried to tell him. And the Grandmother tried to tell him. But they were all crying so hard that he could not understand what they were trying to say.

Then the Grandfather looked into the mirror. He became very angry.

"What a bad son I have," cried the Grandfather. "To think that he would bring another old man into his house while I was still alive."

Just then Mr. Kim came into the room.

"What is the matter?" cried Mr. Kim who had never before heard such crying in his own house.

Then Cho, his wife, who was a strong woman, took Mr. Kim by the hair. She pulled him out of the house. Up the street she went. The three daughters and the Grandmother and the Grandfather followed her. And all Mr. Kim could say was, "What is the matter? What is the matter?"

At last Cho came to the house of the

Judge. She took Mr. Kim before the Judge. She told the Judge what a bad thing Mr. Kim had done to bring someone into their house.

Then the Judge spoke to Mr. Kim.

"What have you done to have caused your wife to be so angry?" asked the Judge.

"It must be the 'round magic' that I bought in Seoul," said Mr. Kim. "There is a man in the 'round magic.'"

"No, No," cried Cho the wife. "He brought a woman to our home."

"No, No," said the daughter. "It was a young girl."

Then the Grandfather who was carrying the mirror went up to the Judge and said, "Look for yourself. You can see that it was an old man that my son brought back from Seoul."

The Judge had never seen a mirror

before. And when he looked into the mirror, he did not see an old man. He saw another judge. He became very angry and he cried out,

"What do you people mean by bringing another Judge into my house?"

Just then a servant came in and told the Judge that a man was at the door. He had come all the way from Seoul with a letter from the King.

"Surely," cried poor Mr. Kim, "This man from Seoul can tell us what this 'round magic' is."

And so when the King's man came in, the Judge bowed low and said,

"Kind Sir, will you please tell us what this 'round magic' is that makes us all so angry."

The King's man, who knew all about mirrors, told these good people what a mirror really was. Then how the Judge laughed. And how Mr. Kim laughed.

And the Grandfather laughed. Now when a Korean starts to laugh, it is sometimes hard for him to stop. They must have laughed half an hour.

The girls wanted to look into the mirror. They did not know that they had such pretty faces. But the Grandmother said that all old women looked just alike and she would not look into the mirror again. And Cho, the wife bowed low before Mr. Kim and said,

"Please forgive me. I shall never be angry with you again."

"And now go home," said the Judge. "Remember that you are never going to be angry again. "

So Mr. and Mrs. Kim and the daughters and the Grandmother and the Grandfather went home. They asked all their friends to come and see the mirror. And after that everyone in the village wanted a mirror.

# The Story of the Stone Lion

At the foot of the mountains of Tibet, an old woman lived on a farm with her two sons. As the father was dead, the two brothers worked the farm for their mother.

Now the older brother was a very bright man but he was not kind. And the younger brother was slow and not very bright. But he was very kind and everyone liked him.

The older brother took care of all the family money. He looked after the farm and did all the buying and selling. And he came to feel that everything belonged to him.

The younger brother was quite willing to help, but he was so slow that the older brother did not like to have him around.

One day, the older brother called his younger brother to him and said, "I am tired of doing everything for this family while you do nothing at all. You must leave here now and go out and work for your own living."

This made the younger brother very sad. But he got ready to leave. He put his clothes in a bag and went to say good-bye to his mother.

The mother was very angry when she heard the news.

"Very well," she said. "If your brother says that you must leave, I will go with you. I will not stay and keep house for such an unkind man."

And so the mother and the younger son left the house together. They had not gone far until they found an empty house at the foot of the mountains. It was not far from a town.

"No one seems to be living in this

house," said the old woman. "Let us sleep here tonight. And tomorrow we can go into the town and find work."

Early the next morning, the young man got up and looked around him. Seeing an ax by the door, he took it and went out into the woods. He cut wood and before long he had a lot of wood ready.

He took it into the town and sold it. This was the first money the younger son had ever had. He hurried back to the little house to show it to his mother.

"Look, Mother, look!" he cried. "I cut wood and sold it in the town. I got all this money for my work. Now I know that I can make enough money to buy what we need and you will never go hungry."

The next morning, the young man shouldered his ax and went off again. He cut a lot of wood, and then he walked up the mountain to hunt for more.

There in a little open place in the woods, he came upon a stone lion. The lion had been cut out of the stone so carefully that for a minute the young man thought that it was a real lion.

But when the lion did not move, he knew that it really was a stone lion. And he said to himself,

"This stone lion must be the god of this mountain. And tomorrow I will bring him something to show him how thankful I am that he has taken such good care of me."

That day when the younger son had sold his wood in the town, he took some of the money and bought two candles. The next morning, he went straight to the open place where the stone lion stood.

The young man lighted the candles

and put one on each side of the lion. Then he got down on his knees before the lion and thanked the lion for letting him cut the wood on his mountain.

Then to his great surprise, the lion opened his mouth and said, "Who are you, and what are you doing on my mountain?"

As soon as the young man got over his surprise, he said, "I am just a young man who was sent from my home by an older brother. My old mother went with me. I have found that I can earn money to buy food for myself and my mother by cutting wood and selling it in the town. I thought that you, oh great Stone Lion, were the god of this mountain. And I am thanking you for taking such good care of me and my old mother."

"Very good," said the lion. must do as I tell you. Com

this time tomorrow. Bring with you a large empty pail.''

The young man said that he would come next morning with a pail. And then he hurried away to sell his wood in the town. With some of the money, he bought a large wooden pail.

The next morning, he took the pail and went up the mountain to where the stone lion stood. Again he bowed low before the stone lion and said,

"I am here again and I have brought you a large wooden pail.''

"Very good," said the stone lion. "And now you must do just as I tell you. Hold your pail under my mouth. I will fill it with gold for you and your mother so that you will never want for money again. But when the pail is nearly full, cry 'Stop' for not one piece of gold must fall upon the ground.''

The young man did just as the stone

lion had told him to do. He held the pail under the lion's mouth and out came the gold pieces. When the pail was nearly full, he cried "Stop," and the gold stopped coming. And not one piece of gold fell upon the ground.

"Thank you, Thank you, Oh Great Stone Lion of the Mountain," said the young man and he hurried home to show the pail full of gold pieces to his mother.

The very next day the younger son bought a good farm with a fine house upon it. He bought many sheep and cows. The mother and the son lived on the farm and were very happy. They always had everything that they wanted. And the younger son took such good care of the farm that it was the finest farm in all the country around.

# The Stone Lion and the Older Brother

After the younger son and his mother had been driven from their home by the older son, they found the stone lion in the woods on the mountain. The stone lion had given the younger brother a pail of gold pieces. With these, the younger brother bought himself a fine farm.

It was not long until the news of this fine farm came to the ears of the older brother. He had married a good wife and had a little son. One day he said to his wife,

"I want my mother to see her little grandson. Get the child ready and we will go and see my younger brother. I want to see this fine farm that I am hearing about."

The old mother was very glad to see her little grandson. And she said to the younger brother,

"Let what is past stay in the past. Be friends with your older brother and his wife." And so the family had a nice visit together.

The older brother wanted to know how his younger brother had made so much money. And it was not long before the older brother knew all about the stone lion on the mountain and the wooden pail of gold pieces.

That night when he went to his own house, he said to his wife,

"If that slow fellow can get that much money from a stone lion, a bright fellow like me should get much more."

The next morning the older brother went into town and bought the largest wooden pail that he could find. And then he bought two candles. He started for the mountain. At last he found the open place where the stone lion stood.

He lighted the two candles and placed them on each side of the lion. Then he bowed down before the stone lion.

"Great Stone Lion," said the older brother. "I want to thank you for all the good you have done my family."

"Who are you," said the Stone Lion. "And what good have I done your family?"

"I am the brother of the young man who came to you a few years ago. You gave him a pail of gold pieces and now he has the finest farm in the country. And I have come to ask you to give me a pail of gold pieces, too."

"Very good," said the stone lion. "And now you must do just as I tell you. Hold your pail under my mouth. I will fill it with gold. But when the pail is nearly full, cry 'Stop,' for not one piece of gold must fall upon the ground."

So the older brother put his pail under the lion's mouth and the gold began to fall into it. He shook the pail so that it could hold more gold. And when the pail was nearly full, he did not say "Stop," for he wanted more and more of the gold. At last the pail was so full that one piece of gold fell on the ground.

The gold stopped coming from the lion's mouth. The older brother said, "Is that all the gold you have? Do you not have any more?"

Then the stone lion said, "The largest piece of gold is still in my throat. Put your hand into my mouth and pull it out."

The older brother stepped up and put his whole arm into the lion's mouth for he wanted that biggest piece of gold.

Just as he did so, the lion's big stone teeth came together and the man's arm was caught fast.

The older brother pulled and pulled but he could not get his arm out of the stone lion's mouth. He kicked the stone lion and he hurt his foot. He called for help but nobody came.

"Well," the older brother thought, "Pretty soon my wife will come and find me. She will get me out of this. And then we will take home our big pail of gold and live happily ever after." But when he looked down at the pail on the ground, it was filled with dirt and stones. And then the man really did begin to cry.

When her husband did not come home at night, the wife was sure that he had been hurt. Early the next morning she went up the mountain.

And there she found him with his arm in the stone lion's mouth.

"Oh, wife, wife," he cried. "What am I to do. I put my arm into the lion's mouth to get one last piece of gold that he said was there. Just then his teeth came shut and I cannot get my arm out. Oh, what shall I do?"

The poor woman did not know what to do. She bowed down before the stone lion and asked him please to open his mouth. But nothing happened. She picked up a stick and beat the stone lion's head. When he did not move, she hurried home and brought some candles to burn before him. But the stone lion did not move.

At last she gave up. She went home again and brought a coat and some food for her husband.

"I will come tomorrow and bring you food. And I will bring many candles to burn before the stone lion," said the wife. "But now I must go home and look after our baby."

And so for many, many days the poor wife brought food to her husband and many candles to burn before the stone lion. Each day, she bowed down before the lion and asked him to open his teeth. The candles cost much money. But the stone lion did not move.

As there was no one to work upon the farm, there was no more money coming in. And because the food and the candles cost a lot of money, it was not long before the money that the wife had was all gone. Then she began to sell the cows and the sheep to get money with which to buy the food and the candles. Pretty soon, the wife had to sell her tables and her chairs and her beds.

At last the day came when there was

nothing left to sell. That day she brought the child and fell down at her husband's feet.

"I have sold everything that we have to buy food for you and candles for the stone lion. There is nothing left. There is nothing for us to do but to die right here at the feet of the stone lion."

On hearing this, the lion opened his mouth wide. Quickly the older brother pulled his arm out of the lion's mouth. Then he picked up his child and took his wife by the arm and ran down the mountain as fast as he could go. He went at once to the house of his brother and told him the whole story.

The younger brother was kind to him and gave him food and clothing and a place to sleep.

The old mother said to the older son, "My Son, you have always wanted more and more of everything. I hope that the stone lion will help you to remember to be happy with what you have."

The older brother had learned his lesson. From that day on he changed his ways. He lived on the younger brother's farm and helped him all he could. The old woman was very happy. And the whole family lived together the rest of their lives at the foot of the mountains of Tibet.

# The Maker of Puppets

In the country of Indonesia, which is a land of many green islands, there lived a man who made puppets. His name was Ali ben Yunes. He and his wife lived in a little town near a deep woods.

Ali ben Yunes worked in the fields with his water buffalo. And he hunted in the deep woods for animals so that he and his wife would have meat to eat. But most of all, Ali ben Yunes liked to make puppets. He cut them out of wood, and he liked to sing as he made them dance for the children who lived in the little town. Often Ali ben Yunes would make a puppet and give it to one of the children. And that child would be very happy. He never forgot Ali ben Yunes.

Nothing that Ali did pleased his wife. When he was working in the field with his water buffalo, she wanted him to get her some wood to burn. When he went hunting, she did not see why he was not working in the fields. When he played with the children his wife said that he should be working. From morning until night Ali ben Yunes could hear his wife calling, "Where is that man? Where is that man?" Ali ben Yunes worked very hard. He worked all the time. But he could never make his wife happy.

One morning Ali was awakened very early by the singing of the birds. He had been dreaming of such pretty music that he would sing as he made his puppets dance. He wanted to get some wood and make some new puppets. His wife was still sleeping and he did not want to wake her. And so he quietly got out of bed and made for the door. But just as he was going out of the door, he fell over one of his wife's big pots. It made a great noise as it rolled on the floor.

Ali's wife woke up with a start. "Where is that man, where is that man?" she called.

"Here I am," said Ali. "I fell over one of your pots."

"And why are you standing there?" cried his wife. "You and your water buffalo should be out in the field working."

Ali started to go out of the door. But his wife called, "Go and get me some wood. How do you expect me to cook our food without a fire?"

And so Ali took his ax and went into the deep woods. He walked slowly. The sun was coming up and everything looked so beautiful. He thought of the songs that he wanted to sing for his puppets. Ali walked on and on through the deep woods.

The woods got very dark. The trees were so thick that the sun could not shine through them. At last Ali ben Yunes came to a clearing in the woods. There was an open place among the trees. The sun came through, and thick grass grew all around.

Two old men sat under a big tree playing a game. They had a game-board on which there were a lot of little wooden puppets. Ali ben Yunes had never seen such beautiful puppets. He wanted to see the puppets better. He wished he could make some like them. And he wondered what game the two old men played with the puppets.

"My friends," said Ali, "May I stay and watch your game?"

The two old men smiled at Ali but they did not say a word. First one old man would think a long, long time, and then he would move one of the little puppets. Then the other man would think a long, long time, and he would move one of the little puppets. Ali sat beside them on the grass and watched.

Ali sat there a long, long time. The old men played on and on. Each one took a long time to think of what move he would make next. All the while, Ali ben Yunes watched the game. And all the time, he thought how beautiful the puppets were.

At last one of the old men picked up the little puppets and put them into his pocket. The other old man picked up the game-board. They went away into the deep woods. Ali could not see where they had gone.

Ali had been sitting so long that he

could hardly move. At last he got to his feet.

He thought that he had better begin to cut the wood for his wife. He looked around him for his ax. He wondered why the grass had grown so tall. At last he found an ax in the grass. But it looked like an old, old ax.

Ali began to cut some wood. But it was getting very dark and he was afraid he could not find his way through the deep woods. He thought that he had better be getting home. So he took up the wood he had cut and he started home. He had a hard time to find the path.

Ali walked and walked through the deep woods. He came to the little town where he lived just as the sun was going down. He walked up and down the streets but he could not find the house where he had lived.

"I must be dreaming," said Ali to himself. He looked and he looked but his house was not where it should have been.

He looked at the people in the streets but he did not see anybody that he knew. He went to the shop of the man who made silver bells.

"Where is Achmud, the man who makes the silver bells?" asked Ali.

A young man was in the shop and he said,

"Achmud is not here any more. He died a long time ago. He was a very old man."

"No, No, No," cried Ali. "Achmud was a young man. He was about as old as I am."

The young man looked at Ali, and he said, "Master, something must be wrong."

"There is nothing wrong," said Ali.

"I am Ali ben Yunes and I have lived in this town for many years."

"I do not know you," said the young man. "I have never seen you before."

Ali went out of the store. He went up and down the streets of the town saying to everyone that he met,

"I am Ali ben Yunes, the maker of puppets. Where is my wife? I am bringing her some wood so that she can cook our food. And where is my house and my water buffalo?"

But no one knew Ali ben Yunes, the maker of puppets.

At last an old man came up and said, "I remember the name of Ali ben Yunes. When I was a child, he made me a puppet. But Ali ben Yunes went away into the deep woods and never came back. And that was a long, long time ago."

Ali stood with the wood in his arms

and he did not know what to do. And then a very old woman who could hardly see came up and looked into his face.

"There is that man. There is that man," she cried. "Ali ben Yunes, it took you long enough to get me some wood for a fire so that I could cook our food."

Ali was so glad to find his wife that tears came to his eyes. He knew that he must have been in the deep woods a long, long time. Years and years had passed while he watched the two old men play their game of puppets on a board.

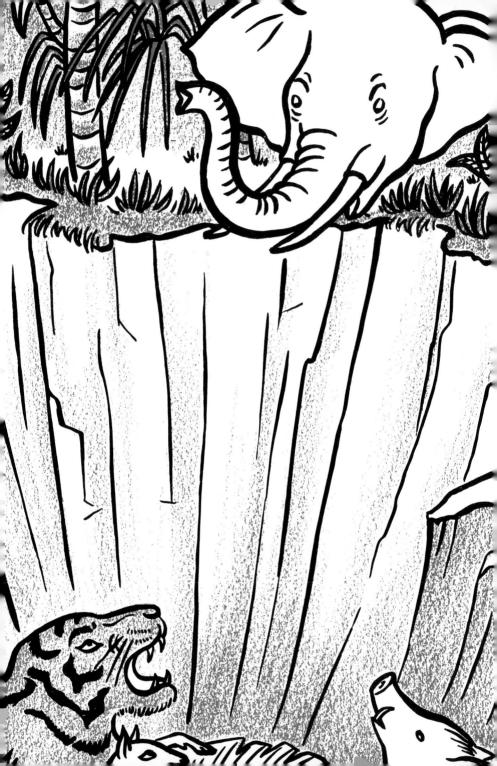

# The Mouse Deer

The children of Indonesia like best the stories about Kantchil, the Mouse Deer. The Mouse Deer is only a foot high. He lives in the woods with other animals who are big and wild like the tiger and the elephant. But the little Mouse Deer can take care of himself.

One day Kantchil was walking down the road. As he passed a Farmer's house, he smelled a good smell. Kantchil walked up to the house and looked in at the door. There was no one in the house but there on the table was a cake that had just been baked. It was set out on some banana leaves to cool. Kantchil went into the house and took the cake. He wrapped it in the banana leaves and then he went on with his walk.

As he walked, Kantchil opened the banana leaves and took a bite of the cake. It was very good. As he walked he ate more and more of the cake. He did not watch where he was going. Before he knew it, Kantchil, the Mouse Deer, fell into the Farmer's lime pit.

The lime pit was a deep hole where the Farmer burned the lime stone and made the white lime to put on his fields. The pit was very, very big and very deep. And Kantchil did not know how he was ever going to get out of it.

Pretty soon Kantchil heard an animal at the top of the lime pit.

"Ah yes," said Kantchil out loud. "This is the very word of the gods." Then he looked up and saw the head of a wild pig looking over the edge of the lime pit.

"Who is talking about gods down there?" asked the wild pig.

Kantchil looked at the big banana leaf that had been around his cake. He acted as if he were reading from it.

"Hear, hear," he called. "The gods have said it. This is the last day for most of the animals in the world. Only those animals who hide in the lime pit will live through the day."

"Who says so?" asked the Wild Pig.

"Can you not hear what I am reading?" said Kantchil. "Just listen to this–," and he went on as if he were reading from the banana leaf.

"On such and such a day, which is today, the world will come to an end. Only those animals who are hiding in the lime pit shall be left alive."

"Is that really so?" asked the Wild Pig.

"Would you question the word of the gods?" asked Kantchil.

"Oh, no, no, no," said the Wild Pig.

"But if that is so, I think that I had better jump down into the lime pit with you."

"No, that will not do," said Kantchil. "It says here that only those animals who never sneeze may get into the lime pit. You are always sneezing and so you must not jump down. You must stay up there until the end of the world."

"I will not sneeze," said the Wild Pig. "Oh, please let me come down into the lime pit with you. I will not sneeze."

"It says here in the very words of the gods," said Kantchil, "that anyone who sneezes must be thrown out of the lime pit."

"I will not sneeze," said the Wild Pig. And he jumped down into the lime pit.

Pretty soon, a Tiger looked down into the lime pit.

"Do I hear someone talking down there?" he asked.

"Yes, Yes," cried the Wild Pig. "The world is coming to an end today. Kantchil has read it. Those are the very words of the gods. And all the animals who are not in the lime pit will die."

"Well, I guess that I had better jump down into the lime pit with you," said the Tiger.

"No, No," cried the Wild Pig. "You must not jump down. You are always sneezing."

"Now what does sneezing have to do with my jumping down into the lime pit?" asked the Tiger.

Kantchil looked at the big banana leaf and acted as if he were reading from it.

"The word of the gods says, 'He who

sneezes must be thrown out of the lime pit.' "

"I will not sneeze," said the Tiger. "Oh, please let me jump down into the lime pit with you. I am sure that I will not sneeze." And he jumped down into the lime pit.

Just then there was the sound of heavy feet. A big Elephant looked down into the lime pit.

"Why are you all hiding down there?" asked the Elephant.

"The world is coming to an end today," said the Tiger. "Only those animals who are hiding in the lime pit will be left alive."

"Well," said the Elephant. "I think that I will come down into the lime pit with you."

"No, No, No," they all cried. "You are too big in the first place. And in the second place you are always sneezing.

You sneeze very often and very loud."

"Now what has sneezing got to do with my getting into the lime pit?" asked the Elephant.

"It is so written," said Kantchil, "that anyone who sneezes must be thrown out of the lime pit."

"I will not sneeze," said the Elephant. "Get out of my way for I am coming down into the lime pit."

The Elephant was so big that he nearly filled the lime pit. The other animals had to sit very close together. Kantchil sat by himself and looked at the banana leaf as if he were reading from it.

Then he looked up at the Elephant. "Get out of here!" he cried loudly. "Get out of here! You look as if you were going to sneeze."

"I am not going to sneeze," cried the Elephant. "See here, I sneeze through my trunk which is really my nose. I will put my foot on it so that I can't sneeze." So the Elephant put his big foot on the end of his trunk.

Kantchil went on looking at the banana leaf as if he were reading. Soon he looked up at the Tiger.

"What was that," he asked. "Did I hear you sneeze?"

"No," said the Tiger. "I did not sneeze. I only rubbed my nose."

Then Kantchil got a funny look upon his face. He took hold of his nose.

"Oh, no, no," he cried. "I must not sneeze! Oh–Oh–achoo–achoo." And Kantchil sneezed a great big sneeze.

"He has done it," cried the other animals. "The Mouse Deer has sneezed. Out he goes."

So all together, they took hold of the little Mouse Deer and threw him out of the lime pit.

"Oh, thank you," cried Kantchil, the Mouse Deer, as he ran away. "Thank you very much for helping me out of the lime pit. Now you get out as best you can!"

And he ran away laughing.

# The Stone Crusher

Ismail ben Aland was a stone crusher. All of his life he had lived on the side of a mountain. Every morning he took his hammer and went up the mountain side. He pounded away at the rocks with his hammer. By noon he had broken some big rocks into little rocks. He put the little rocks into a bag and took them into the city to sell.

One day when Ismail got to the city, he was very tired. The sun had been very hot. He sat down under a tree to rest. There was a knife maker sitting under the tree, and the two men began to talk. The knife maker who was young and strong said to Ismail,

"Don't you think that crushing stone is very hard work for a man as old as you are?"

"All my life I have been a stone crusher," said Ismail. "I want to crush stone to the end of my days. A stone crusher is the strongest thing in the world."

"Yes, yes," said the young man. "But what is stronger than the blacksmith who makes knives?"

And then Ismail ben Alang told the maker of knives the story of the young stone crusher who lived on the side of the mountain.

One day the stone crusher was walking through the streets of the city with his bags of stones. He looked up at the palace of the Rajah, or king. And there he saw the Rajah and the Rani, or queen, playing a game. They were dressed in beautiful clothes and they had nothing else to do but to sit in the sun and play a game.

"Oh," said the young stone crusher

to himself. "There is nothing in all the world as strong and as great as a Rajah. I wish that I could be a Rajah and sit in the sun and play a game."

Suddenly the young stone crusher was in a palace sitting in the sun playing a game with the Rani.

"It is your play," said the Rani.

"No," said the young stone crusher. "It is your play."

The sun was shining down upon them and the young stone crusher became very hot.

"I thought that the Rajah was the strongest thing in the world," said the young stone crusher to himself. "But the sun can burn a Rajah. I would like to be the sun so that I could burn the skin of a Rajah."

The young stone crusher became the sun. The sun made the earth hot. And everywhere the sun found a Rajah, the sun burned the skin of the Rajah a dark brown.

"Now, I am the strongest thing in the world," said the sun.

But a little cloud came and shut off the sun from the earth.

"Oh," cried the sun. "A little cloud is stronger than I am, for it can stop me from making the earth hot. I wish that I were a little cloud."

Then the young stone crusher became a little cloud. He was very happy. But pretty soon the wind came and blew the little cloud away. And the little cloud could do nothing about it.

"Oh, dear," said the little cloud. "The wind is stronger than I am. I believe the wind must be the strongest thing in the world. I wish that I were the wind."

And so the young stone crusher became the wind. And what a good time the wind had. It blew the clouds around. It blew the trees and shook their leaves. It blew the ocean into great waves. But suddenly the wind came to the mountains. And the wind could not blow away the mountain.

"Oh, dear, dear," said the wind. "What am I to do. I have to blow around the mountain. The mountain is the strongest thing in the world. If only I could be a mountain, I would be happy."

The young stone crusher became a mountain. And he stood with his head in the clouds. He was very happy.

But a man came up the sides of the mountain. He carried a hammer. He broke rock from the mountain side and he crushed the rock into little pieces. He put the little pieces of rock into bags and carried them to the city and sold them.

"I did not understand," said the mountain. "A small man can crush me piece by piece. He must be the strongest thing in the world. If only I could go back to being a stone crusher, I would never ask for anything else as long as I live."

The young stone crusher found himself on the mountain side with his hammer. He crushed the rocks into little pieces. And he put the little pieces into bags and took them to the city. He walked by the palace and saw the Rajah and the Rani playing their game. And the stone crusher laughed to himself.

Then Ismail looked at the maker of knives and said,

"It is true that I am an old man now. But I am happy. For I know that a stone crusher is the strongest thing in the world. When I was young, I learned that the sun can burn the

Rajah though the Rajah is great and strong. But the cloud can shut off the sun. And the wind can blow the cloud away. I learned that the mountain stops the wind. But I also learned that the stone crusher is the strongest, for only he can crush the mountain."

# The Tiger, the Brahman, and the Jackal

Once upon a time in India a Tiger was caught in a cage. He jumped and he jumped but he could not get out of the cage.

At last a man called a Brahman came by and the Tiger cried out,

"Oh, good and kind Brahman, let me out of this cage or I shall die."

The Brahman stopped and said to the Tiger,

"Tiger, Tiger, if I should let you out of that cage, you would eat me."

"No, No, No," cried the Tiger. "If you let me out of this cage, I will be your servant and do what you say all my life," and big tears rolled out of the Tiger's eyes.

The Brahman felt so sorry for the Tiger that he opened the door of the cage and let the Tiger out.

The Tiger was no sooner out of the cage than he said to the Brahman,

"I have been in that cage a long time and I am very hungry. I think that I will eat you."

But the Brahman talked to the Tiger and said,

"It is not right that you should eat me. I let you out of the cage and you said that you would be my servant."

But the Tiger still said that he was so hungry that he was going to eat the Brahman.

"It is not for us to say," said the Brahman. "We must ask of three what they think. And if two of them say that it is right that you should eat me,

I, the Brahman, will lie down in the grass and let you, the Tiger, eat me."

"All right," said the Tiger. "Ask of three and see what they say."

And so the Brahman first asked a pipal tree what he thought of the matter.

"Do you think that it is right that the Tiger should eat me?" asked the Brahman, after he had told his story.

"There is no right in the world," said the pipal tree. "Just look at me. I grow my branches and my beautiful leaves. Men and animals stand under me to get away from the hot sun. But what do men do to me? They break my branches and they shake my beautiful leaves down to feed their cows. There is no right in the world."

The Brahman's heart was very heavy but he went on until he found a water buffalo. He told him how he had let the Tiger out of the cage, and how the Tiger had said that he would be his servant. But now that the Tiger was out of the cage he wanted to eat the Brahman.

"Do you think that this is right that the Tiger should eat me?" asked the Brahman.

"There is no right in the world," said the water buffalo. "When I was young, I stayed on a farm. Everyone thought that I was a fine animal. I was given good food to eat. But look at me now. I am old and I have to pull this big wheel around and around. No one brings me any good food now. I have only the grass that grows in the field to eat."

The Brahman was sorry for the old water buffalo. He gave him some green leaves to eat. And then he started to walk back to where the Tiger was waiting for him. And on the way, he met a Jackal.

"Mr. Brahman, Mr. Brahman," called the Jackal. "What is the matter? You look as happy as a fish out of water."

The Brahman sat down and he told the Jackal about how he let the Tiger out of the cage. He told the Jackal that the pipal tree and the water buffalo had said that there was no right in the world. He told the Jackal that he was going back to the Tiger, and lie down in the grass so that the Tiger could eat him.

"Well, Well, Well," said the Jackal. "Would you mind telling me the story all over again for I do not understand."

The Brahman told the story all over again. But the Jackal shook his head.

"It is all very funny," said the Jackal. "The story seems to go into one of my ears and out the other. Let us go back to where the story began."

And so the Brahman and the Jackal went back to where the Tiger was waiting.

"You have been away a long time," said the Tiger. "I am very hungry and I want to eat you."

The Brahman was very much afraid, but he said to the Tiger,

"Let me have just five minutes so that I can tell the Jackal the whole story again."

"All right," said the Tiger, "but be quick about it for I am hungry."

The Brahman told the Jackal the whole story again.

"Oh dear, Oh dear," said the Jackal. "My head goes round and round. But I want to get the story just right. You were in the cage and the Tiger came walking by."

"No, No," said the Tiger, "I was in the cage."

"Of course, of course," said the Jackal. "I was in the cage. No, No, I was not in the cage. Oh, my poor head. It goes round and round. Let me see. . . . The Tiger was in the Brahman and the cage came walking by. That was how it was.

"No, No," said the Tiger. "I will make you understand. Look at me. I am the Tiger."

"Yes, Master Tiger," said the Jackal.

"And that is the Brahman."

"Yes, Master Tiger."

"And over there is the cage."

"Yes, Master Tiger."

"And I was in the cage. Now do you understand?"

"Yes—No, Master Tiger. How did you get into the cage?"

"How did I get into the cage?" cried the Tiger and he was very angry because the Jackal did not understand.

"I got into the cage like this." And the Tiger ran and jumped into the cage.

The Jackal shut the door of the cage and made it fast.

"Oh, yes," laughed the Jackal. "Now I understand. This was where the story began."

The Tiger who would not keep his word was back in the cage where he belonged. He jumped and jumped. He made a great noise. Tears came from his eyes. But no one was sorry for him.

The Brahman thanked the Jackal for saving his life. He said he had never known how smart the Jackal really was. And then he went on his way.

The Jackal ran home. He laughed and laughed and he said to himself, "The Brahman is a very wise man, but he did not get himself out of his trouble. The pipal tree did not help him. The old water buffalo did not help him. People make fun of the Jackal, but at times it takes the Jackal to right a wrong in this world."

# The Mice That Ate the Iron Balance

Once upon a time there was in India a rich storekeeper. He was getting very old and so he called his only son to him and said.

"My dear son, I am getting very old. I know that I will not be with you for long. I want you to be a good store-keeper and take care of the store. Take good care of the iron balance. It tells how much you are to sell and it tells how much you are to buy. Remember to take good care of the iron balance."

Not long after that the storekeeper died.

The son did not think that he wanted to be a storekeeper and so he took his father's money and went off to the big city. But he could not take the iron balance with him. He remembered that his father had told him to take good care of the iron balance. And so he thought that he would leave the iron balance with a friend.

The son had a good time in the city and he spent all of his father's money. And then he said to himself,

"This city is not for me. I must go back to the town where I was born and become a good storekeeper like my father."

The young man went back to the town where he had been born. He went to his friend and said,

"Give me my father's iron balance for I have come back to open a store and become a good storekeeper."

The friend laughed to himself for he wanted to keep the iron balance to use in his own store.

So he said, "I am sorry that I can

not give you the iron balance. While you were away in the city, the mice ate your iron balance."

"The mice ate the iron balance?" cried the young man. "How could mice eat iron? That is not possible."

The friend just shook his head.

"I am sorry," he said. "There are strange mice in this country. I left the iron balance in my store. But when I looked for it again, the iron balance was all eaten up."

The young man did not say anything more, for he knew what his friend was thinking. But the next day, he went to his friend's house and said,

"I have come to play with your little boy. It is a nice day and we can go swimming in the river."

The young man and the little boy had a good time together. But when it was time to go home, the young man took the little boy to the house of an old woman and told the old woman to care for the boy. Then he went alone to his friend's house.

"Where is my little boy?" asked his friend.

"I am sorry," said the young man, "But a big bird flew down from the sky and carried your little boy away."

"What are you saying," cried the friend. "A bird cannot fly away with a child."

"Surely," said the young man, "in a country where the mice could eat an iron balance, a bird could fly away with an elephant. And your son was only a little boy."

Then the friend knew that his trick had been found out. And he knew what he must do to get his son back.

"I am sorry that I did you wrong," said the friend. "I wanted to keep the iron balance for my own store. Go and get my little boy and I will go and get your iron balance."

The young man got back the iron balance his father had left him. He opened a store and he made a very good storekeeper.

# The Brave Pot-Maker

Upon a very stormy night in India, a large tiger wanted to get out of the rain. He came upon the house of an old woman. So he lay down close to the wall where the rain would not get him wet.

The house was old and the roof had many holes in it where the rain came through. The tiger could hear the old woman moving about inside the house.

"Oh, Oh, Oh," cried the old woman. "This dripping, this dripping. I am afraid this dripping will make the roof come down." And the old woman pulled her bed away from where the rain was dripping through the roof.

"I wonder what this 'dripping' is that makes the old woman afraid," thought the tiger to himself. Then he heard the old woman say, "Now if an elephant or a lion or a tiger were to walk into this room, I would not be half as much afraid of them as I am of this dripping." She pulled her table to the other side of the room and it made a great noise.

"My, my, my," said the tiger to himself. "She is more afraid of this 'dripping' than she is of a tiger. And just hear what a noise the dripping makes. A dripping must be something very bad. I am beginning to be afraid myself."

Just then a pot-maker came down the road hunting for his donkey who was lost. In the darkness he saw a large animal against the wall of the old woman's house. The pot-maker thought it was his donkey.

The pot-maker ran up to the tiger and took him by the ear.

"Come home with me at once," he cried. And he began to kick the tiger and beat him with a stick.

"Oh, Oh, Oh," cried the tiger. "The 'dripping' has got hold of my ear. The 'dripping' is hurting me and I am afraid that he is going to kill me."

The tiger was so afraid that he walked right along with the pot-maker. The pot-maker took the tiger home and tied him up to a tree in the yard. Then the pot-maker went inside the house.

"I am glad I found that animal tonight," said the pot-maker to his wife. "I could not carry my pots to town without my donkey."

"Well, take off your wet clothes," said his wife, "and let us get some sleep."

And the poor tiger out in the rain was so afraid that he did not make a sound.

"Oh dear, what shall I do," said the tiger to himself. "That 'dripping' is surely going to kill me."

The next morning, the wife looked out of the window and she saw a tiger tied to the tree in the yard .

"Wake up, Wake up," she called to the pot-maker. "Do you know what kind of an animal you brought home last night?"

"Yes," said the pot-maker. "It was my donkey who was lost. I brought him home and tied him to the tree in the yard."

"Come and see," said his wife. "You have tied a tiger to the tree in the yard."

Before long all the people in the town came to see the brave pot-maker. No one had ever heard of a man who was brave enough to catch a tiger and tie him to a tree in his yard. And so someone wrote to the Rajah, which is what they call a King in India, and told him the news.

The Rajah had never heard of a man brave enough to catch a tiger and tie him up in his yard. And so the Rajah and all his men got on their horses and came to see the pot-maker.

Now the tiger was a very large one. And the people of the town told the Rajah how this big tiger had killed many cows and horses. Many people had tried to kill this tiger. But it took the brave pot-maker to catch him and tie him up.

"The pot-maker is the bravest man that I have ever heard of," said the Rajah. "I will give him much money and a fine farm and many horses."

And that was how the pot-maker became a rich man.

# How the Pot-Maker
# Beat the Enemy

It was not long after this that a King in another country made war upon the Rajah. The Rajah did not know what to do, for his soldiers were not ready to fight.

"Who will lead my soldiers against the enemy and save our country?" said the Rajah. But not one of his men spoke up. And the Rajah was very sad.

Then one man said, "Great Rajah, the bravest man in the country should be the leader of your soldiers."

"And who is the bravest man in the country?" asked the Rajah.

Then the man said, "The bravest man in the country is the pot-maker who caught the tiger and tied him to a tree in the yard."

"Very well," said the Rajah, "I will make the pot-maker the leader of my soldiers."

The Rajah sent for the pot-maker and made him the leader of his soldiers.

"The enemy is marching against our country," said the Rajah. "You, the bravest man in the country, are to ride at the head of my soldiers. Go and save our country."

"So be it," said the pot-maker. "But first let me go by myself and see where the enemy is camped."

Then the pot-maker went home to his wife, and said,

"My dear wife, all is lost. An enemy is marching against our country. And the Rajah has made me the leader of his soldiers. I will have to ride at the head of his soldiers. And you know that I have never been on a horse."

"My poor husband," said his wife, "what are you going to do?"

"I have asked the Rajah to let me go by myself and see where the enemy is camped," said the pot-maker. "Goodbye, dear wife. I will go now but I may never come back."

Just then one of the Rajah's men rode up to the door leading a beautiful big horse.

"The Rajah has sent you one of his finest horses," said the man to the pot-maker. "He wants you to bring him news of where the enemy is camped as quickly as you can." And then the man rode away.

"What shall I do?" said the pot-maker to his wife. "I cannot ride this big horse."

"Dear husband," said the wife, "you must ride the horse that the Rajah sent to you. If you don't, the Rajah might kill you. I will tie you onto the horse so that you will not fall off."

"But how can I get onto the horse?" asked the pot maker.

"You must jump," said his wife.

The pot-maker jumped and he jumped. At last he got on the back of the horse, but he was facing the horse's tail.

"No, No, No," said his wife. "When you are on a horse, you must face the horse's head."

And so the pot-maker got down and tried all over again. At last the pot-maker got on the back of the horse again and this time he was facing the horse's head.

The wife took a long rope and tied him onto the horse. She tied his feet. And she tied his legs. And she put the rope around his body many times. She tied her husband to the big horse.

But the horse did not like all of this rope being tied around him. At last he would stand still no longer. He was off across the country like the wind.

"You did not tie my hands," cried the pot-maker.

"Hold on, Hold on," cried his wife. Never had she seen a horse that could run so fast.

Away went the horse. And away went the pot-maker. The big horse ran and ran. He went over the fields and through the rivers. At last he came to a big field where the enemy were camped.

When the pot-maker saw the big camp of the enemy, he said to himself,

"Now all is lost. For when this horse rides into the enemy's camp, I will be killed." And the pot-maker reached up and took hold of the branches of a tree to try and stop the horse. But the horse was so strong that he just pulled and the tree came right out of the ground.

The big horse ran into the enemy's camp. And the pot-maker sat on the horse's back, for his wife had tied him very well, holding a tree in his hands.

When the soldiers in the camp saw the horse and man coming, they were afraid. They had never seen anything like this before.

"The great Rajah is coming and he is as tall as a tree," the soldiers cried. "The great Rajah is coming to kill us." And the soldiers ran away as fast as they could go. And their King could not get them to stop.

So the King wrote a letter to the Rajah telling him that he would not fight. And then the King got on his horse and rode away after his soldiers.

Just as the pot-maker rode up to the King's tent, the ropes which had held for so long, broke and the poor pot-maker fell to the ground. He picked himself up and went into the King's tent. And there he found the letter that the King had written to his Rajah telling him that the enemy would not fight.

The pot-maker took the letter, and leading his horse, for he was afraid to get up on the horse again, he went back to his home.

"Dear wife,'" said the pot-maker, "since I saw you last, I have been around the world and I am very tired. The enemy of our Rajah has gone and I must go to bed. Please send this letter and this horse back to the Rajah."

The wife sent the letter and the beautiful big horse back to the Rajah. And when the Rajah read the letter, he said,

"Never have I known a man as brave as the pot-maker. All by himself, he has made our enemy go home. I will make the pot-maker the richest man in the country."

And the pot-maker became the richest man in the country. But never again did he ride upon a horse.